E
C.4

Zinnemann-Hope, Pam
  Time for bed Ned. Illus. by Kady
MacDonald Denton.   Margaret K.
McElderry Books, 1986.
  n.p. col. illus.

I. Title.

For Carolyn Dinan

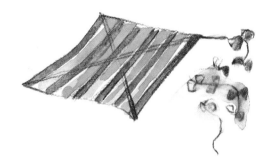

Text copyright © 1986 by Pam Zinnemann-Hope
Illustrations copyright © 1986 by Kady MacDonald Denton
All rights reserved
Published by Margaret K. McElderry Books, Macmillan Publishing Company, New York.
Printed in Italy
10   9   8   7   6   5   4   3   2   1
ISBN 0-689-50415-2
Library of Congress catalog card number: 86-61429

FIRST AMERICAN EDITION

Time for Bed

NED

Written by Pam Zinnemann-Hope

Illustrated by Kady MacDonald Denton

E
C. 4

MARGARET K. McELDERRY BOOKS
NEW YORK

"Ned."

"Time for bed, Ned."

Bed, I said."

"No. Not bed."

"Come on, Ned."

"Away we go."

"Go! Go!

"Bath and bed," Mom said.

"Splash in the bath," said Ned.

"Into bed, Ned."

"Good night, Mom," Ned said.